THIS BOOK BELONGS TO

LITTLE SIMON

An imprint of Simon & Schuster Children's Publishing Division

1230 Avenue of the Americas, New York, New York 10020

This Little Simon hardcover edition September 2021

Copyright © 1968, 1996 by Michael Brown

Originally published by Grosset & Dunlap.

For information about special
discounts for bulk purchases, please contact Simon & Schuster Special Sales
at 1-866-506-1949 or business@simonandschuster.com.

The Simon & Schuster Speakers Bureau can bring authors to your live event.
For more information or to book an event contact the Simon & Schuster Speakers Bureau
at 1-866-248-3049 or visit our website at www.simonspeakers.com.

Design by Laura Roode • Title lettering by Angela Navarra

Manufactured in China 0721 SCP

2 4 6 8 10 9 7 5 3

CIP data for this book is available from the Library of Congress.

ISBN 978-1-5344-3802-6 (hc)

ISBN 978-1-5344-3805-7 (eBook)

SANTA MOUSE,
WHERE ARE YOU?

by MICHAEL BROWN
illustrated by ELFRIEDA DE WITT

LITTLE SIMON
New York London Toronto Sydney New Delhi

Ev'ry year, when it's December,
we're excited as can be,
for that's when we remember
it is time to get a tree.

We don't want a tree too tiny
or too tall to fit the house;
the tree we want has got to be
just right for Santa Mouse.

SANTA MOUSE
is Santa's helper.

He goes with him ev'ry year,
and it really isn't Christmas

unless both
of them
appear.

Santa brings big presents in
that come for you and me,
while Santa Mouse takes tiny
gifts and climbs up in the tree.

He puts them right next to the trunk
or way out on a limb.
(If a gift is in the branches,
then we know it came from him!)

Now, once upon a time, someone
who looked a lot like you
was putting lights upon a tree,
some green, some red, some blue.

When suddenly this person said,
"You know what there should be?
A light right at the very top,
so Santa Mouse can see!"

It took a little help, of course,
to set that special light,
but finally, when bedtime came,
it looked exactly right.

Away up high, above the rest,
it shed a gentle beam,
and when little eyes grew sleepy,
it was shining in a dream.

Now, far off, in his workshop,
Santa Mouse was wrapping toys.
He was hurrying to finish
lots of things for girls and boys.

As he hunted for a ribbon,
suddenly this happy fellow
gave a whistle of surprise,
because he found one that was yellow.

He had needed something special
for a very special present,

but then a voice called him,
very deep, yet very pleasant . . .

"It's time to travel, Santa Mouse!
You know we can't be late!"
And Santa stepped into his sleigh.
"Come on, the deer won't wait!"

So Santa Mouse came running
with his present at his side,
and he leaped for Santa's shoulder—
it was time for them to ride.

Off they flew, as fast as lightning—
Santa Mouse was holding on.
But he felt his gift was slipping,
then, my goodness, it was gone!

He said, "Stop!" and tried to save it;
at that moment, off he fell.
But old Santa didn't know it,
and the sleigh went on pell-mell.

He was falling, calling, "Santa!"
But with darkness all around,
there was no one there to hear him—
he was headed for the ground!

Till he thought what he was holding,
tucked his whiskers in his suit,
took the paper and the ribbon
and produced a parachute!

Then KERPLUNK!
He hit a snowbank
and disappeared
from sight,

but he crawled out with his gift
and looked around him in the night.

What he thought was, "I am lost—
everything is cold and bare.
The thing to do is find a house
and wait for Santa there."

But he found nothing but the wind
that chilled him through and through.
It seemed to whisper, "Santa Mouse,
where ARE you, where are YOU?"

"Here I am!" he shouted bravely
as he trudged on through the storm,
holding tightly to his present
as if that could keep him warm.

He sat down and with a sniffle
tied the ribbon in a bow.
Then he noticed something funny—
on the bow there was a glow.

Somewhere near, a light was shining!
He jumped up, and it was true,
for a tiny, golden glimmering
was gleaming through the blue.

Remember how one special light
was placed for Santa Mouse?
He could see it now—it lit the way
for him to reach the house.

He crept inside, and climbed up high
to place it in the tree,
then went to sleep to wait
for Santa Claus, like you and me.

And that's where Santa found him
late that night upon his way.
He picked him up and kissed him
and then tucked him in his sleigh.

So this year, when it is Christmas
and you decorate your tree,
why not put one light upon it
that's as high up as can be?

You may find a tiny present
Christmas morning in your house.
If it's tied with yellow ribbon,
then who brought it?

SANTA MOUSE!